HEATHCLIFF LENNOX

France 1918

Karen Baugh
MENUHIN

ISBN: 978-1-9162947-5-2

CHAPTER 1

Spring 1918. Somewhere in France

'Greggs?'

No reply.

'Greggs, are you all right?'

Still no reply. I was hanging upside down in the remains of my Sopwith Camel, suspended by my straps and spattered in aviation fuel. Greggs, my batman, had been behind me in the trainer seat, not that it was a training flight. We were shifting HQ and I was shuttling him to our new base. Or that had been the plan.

'Sir...' a voice quavered, faint with shock.

'Where are you?'

'I believe you have crashed the aeroplane, sir.'

'Are you hurt?'

'My back, sir... rather sore.' His voice held a tremor of reprimand. 'I was thrown out.'

'Can you move?' I called.

'I believe so, sir.'

Huffing and puffing came from somewhere beyond the

1

wreckage that was shielding my view of a water meadow somewhere in France. The ground was soft with wet grass and damp earth and our attempted landing, and subsequent somersault, had terminated beside the banks of a tumbling brook.

'The carpet bag and contents have fallen out.' Greggs continued. 'Should I go and find…'

'No, would you just come and help, please? And bring a knife.'

'I will be with you…' More huffing was heard. 'Sir! I have found my hat.'

'Marvellous,' I muttered.

Sounds of torn canvas being ripped away, and the heaving and tugging of struts, wires and all the usual materials that made up modern aircraft were heard before Greggs appeared among the debris. 'Good heavens, sir! You are upside down.'

I bit back a sharp retort. 'Yes, thank you, Greggs, where is the knife?'

He passed me a small pocket-knife.

'Is that it?'

'I am afraid all our possessions are scattered about, sir,' he intoned. 'I could pull on the straps?'

'No, I'll do it. You'd better go and keep watch, we're on the wrong side of the lines and someone is bound to have seen us.'

He blanched. 'You mean… Germans, sir?'

'Yes, of course, Germans. Be a good chap and stand guard,' I ordered, then thought of something else. 'And see if you can find the map.'

He shuffled back into the daylight. I was still in the cockpit, the instrument panel was a broken jumble of wires, dials and switches. The small and entirely inadequate windshield was crazed with cracks but hadn't splintered into fragments, for which I was grateful. I sawed at the thick straps holding me in my wicker and leather flying seat, it was heavy going with the ridiculously small penknife and I cursed with every slice.

We'd been enjoying the fresh morning air up in the bright blue sky of France only a short time ago. We'd been ordered to Epiez-sur-Meuse, then told to move again as a new offensive had broken out in the North-West and I was needed at Reims. I'd been promoted to Major because most my fellow officers, and friends, were dead. We were no longer the Royal Flying Corp, we were the Royal Air Force and everything, and nothing, had changed.

The first strap gave way to the blade of the knife, I jerked downwards then jolted to a halt as the other strap caught. Damn it, it hurt. Actually, most of me hurt; it had been a sudden and violent landing caused by a German pilot in an Albatross. He'd dropped out of the clouds and given chase, it was a bit of a shock, I'd been told the German airfields had been grounded by fog. The twin seater I was flying was a trainer and unarmed; I dropped, spun and dodged, but the Boche caught my tail and blasted it to rags with his machine gun. So, now we were in the mud somewhere behind enemy lines and needed to make an escape. I sawed through the remaining strap and fell to the ground.

I crawled out from under the wreckage, cursing under my breath.

'Sausages, sir.' Greggs had been searching the ground among our fallen belongings. 'I found them on the grass by the brook.'

'Did you find the map?'

'I…erm…' he looked around, no doubt the discovery of the sausages had distracted him.

'Right. Well, never mind. Come on, we'll make a dash for it.' I was up and running.

'But… sir, … my back…' Greggs stuttered then broke into a ponderous trot, holding onto his bowler hat. He managed a few yards, then stopped to puff out deep breaths. I hared back to help him, put my arm under his and propelled him through the meadow. I'd have carried him if he hadn't been so damned heavy.

'We'll get to the trees and crawl through the undergrowth, then find somewhere to lie low until nightfall.' I outlined the plan as we stumbled toward a wood, the leaves bright with fresh growth.

'I'm not sure if I could crawl, sir.'

'You can if your life depends on it, Greggs.' We made it into the trees and collapsed behind a fallen log, breathing heavily. I turned over to spy the tangled remains of the plane. 'Boche.'

'Sir?'

'Coming along the bank, over a dozen.' I watched them, uniforms of faded grey walking quickly, rifles held in hands, bayonets glinting in the warm sunshine.

Greggs clutched the paper-wrapped sausages close to his chest, his chins wobbled above his butler's outfit. Despite having a proper batman's uniform, he rarely wore it. I don't think he'd ever entirely accepted that we were subjects of his Majesty's military wing.

'I believe I may be able to crawl after all, sir.'

'Just follow me,' I whispered. I made off at a half crouch, aiming in the opposite direction to the soldiers. My flying Sidcot suit was a hindrance and too hot in the warmth of the day. I considered pulling it off, but decided putting distance between us and them was a higher priority.

We pushed through the undergrowth, caught by thorns and stung by nettles, to reach a track within the woodland. We followed its line and came into a landscape of straggling vines. I headed straight into the densest patch I could find.

'Right, kit off,' I ordered and started to tug at my flying suit.

'All of it?' Greggs looked aghast.

'No, just the jacket, hat and dickie, you can't walk around like that.'

'I am not prepared to relinquish my hat, sir.'

'Greggs, will you…' I wanted to argue, but was already too hot to put up a fight. 'Oh, never mind.'

I'd worn my usual uniform under my flying gear, I ditched the jacket and tie and stopped at shirt, trousers and boots. Greggs wouldn't give up any of it. He couldn't have looked more out of place if he had stripped to the buff.

'We'll go north,' I announced for no good reason and headed off.

We trudged through the vines and reached another track. Logic dictated that where there were tracks there were farms, and farms had food, so we followed the dusty ruts between thick high hedges and arrived at a gate almost hidden in the vegetation. I had a quick look around.

'All clear,' I told him, and climbed over the gate.

'Sir.' He'd tried to follow, and managed to raise himself halfway over. 'I simply cannot…'

'Hande hoch.' A voice shouted, instantly followed by a soldier wielding a rifle with a bayonet attached.

Greggs fell from the gate with a crump.

I pulled my revolver from my belt in an instant and we formed a stand-off; his bayonet inches from my eyes, my barrel aimed at his forehead. Sweat formed on my brow, the German wasn't faring any better; he looked hollow-eyed and haunted. He was probably as sick of this whole stupid mess as we were.

'Sausages,' Greggs shouted. He'd managed to clamber to his feet and held out the package to the soldier.

'Vas?' He seemed surprised, but didn't flinch.

Greggs pulled the wrapping away. 'Sausages,' he repeated.

'Damn it, that's our lunch,' I muttered through gritted teeth.

'This is an emergency, sir.'

The soldier eyed the sausages. He was as likely to have

shot me as I was him. His hair was unkempt under the cap, his cheeks were lean and his grey eyes slid from me to the package.

He lowered his rifle, took the sausages carefully by the wrapping and tucked them away inside his jacket. 'Verlassen sie.'

I think that meant clear off, so we did, at a speed quite remarkable for my portly butler

CHAPTER 2

A deserted farmyard lay at the end of the lane and brought instant cheer to us both. Chickens ran in all directions as we approached, a cockerel crowed from a barnyard roof and I heard the distinct moo of a cow. I wondered how the German soldier had missed this, or was he a deserter? There were many of them now, demoralised and betrayed by their lunatic leadership who refused to recognise that they were beaten.

'Eggs, Greggs, and chicken for dinner.' I clapped my hands and strode across the cobbled yard.

A farmhouse with raddled thatch and broken windows formed one part of a square. Sheep sheds, cow byres, pig-styes and fodder stores formed the remainder. It must have been a cosy spot until the war broke over it – backed by tall trees, terraced vines and sunlit hills beyond. I made for the house and pushed the warped door aside. The smell of ripening cheese greeted me at the threshold, which should have been warning enough.

'Mains en l'air,' a voice growled.

I sighed and turned about to find the sharpened tines

of a pitchfork aimed at my heart. It would have been higher if the old man had been taller, or the handle longer. Chest height was still a sufficient threat though, so I did as ordered and raised my hands.

'Ah, sir,' Greggs called. 'It seems the farm is not deserted.'

'Thank you, Greggs.'

'I have the eggs, but…' He clutched his hat, which was piled with dark brown eggs.

A wizened old lady had shuffled over to him and held out a basket. She waited while he placed them into it, one by one.

'Allez,' the ancient farmer prodded the pitchfork in my direction. He had the look of a pickled walnut, marinaded in brandy; deeply weathered, grizzled of hair and chin, bow-legged and mostly toothless.

'I'm English. I'm on your side.' I tried reason. It didn't work.

'Allez,' he repeated.

'I think he wants you to move, sir,' Greggs said in his helpful manner.

The old lady, as short and bent as her husband, suddenly started shouting something incomprehensibly French at Greggs. He took a hasty step in my direction.

We were herded toward a cow byre as decrepit as the place and people, and continued the retreat until we backed against the far wall of the building. An animated discussion between the ancients ensued, then they shuffled off outside, the old man pausing to swing the door shut and bar it with a loud bang.

'Absolutely marvellous,' I remarked and sat on a large heap of loose straw.

'If you hadn't crashed, sir...'

'I didn't crash, Greggs, we were cut down by a German pilot,' I retorted, stung.

'But if we'd flown nearer the trees,' he continued. 'Which I had suggested...'

'How often have you flown into battle?'

'As you know sir, it is not my task.' He became stuffy. 'Particularly given my years,'.

'And your girth,' I reminded him. 'And you weren't thrown out of the plane, you fell out because you weren't strapped in.'

He sniffed, I'd scored a hit. I knew very well that he'd taken his belt off because it was too tight about his plump form and he hadn't been able to fix it back on again when the Boche launched the attack.

'This is not productive, sir,' he replied huffily.

He was right, so we both shut up and looked about. We wouldn't have any trouble escaping, one good kick to the wall behind us would cause its collapse.

'We'll stay here until nightfall,' I proposed.

'Very well, sir.' He regarded the other inhabitant of the byre. 'We could acquire some milk.'

The cow looked to be the dozy sort. It had barely opened its eyes when we'd been manoeuvred in here. It was imprisoned behind a wooden barrier and rested its brown and white head on the top of the uppermost plank.

'There isn't a bucket,' I mentioned.

'I have my flask, sir.'

'Your hip flask?'

'Indeed, sir.'

'With whisky in it?'

'Jameson's, sir.'

'Hand it over.'

We shared it; it was excellent. Just what the doctor ordered, or would have done if he were with us. I felt much better after that and leaned back against the wall, sinking into the loose straw; there were worse places to wait for dark, I decided.

'Should I attempt some milk, sir?' Greggs sounded slightly slurred.

'Flask empty?'

'To the last drop... hic, sir.'

'Right, give it a go, old chap,' I encouraged him. I doubt he'd ever milked a cow in his life, but strong liquor on an empty stomach does strange things to a man.

He tottered over and gazed at the beast for some moments, then tottered back.

'There is something amiss, sir.'

'What?'

'It is not a cow.'

'Hum,' I contemplated going to look, but decided to take his word for it. 'It looks like a cow.'

'No udders, sir.'

'Ah.' The penny dropped. 'It's a bull.'

'But it doesn't have a ring in its nose.' He collapsed back into the straw.

'That's not the necessary criteria,' I told him.

He started snoring, I gave him a prod with my elbow. He snuffled and sat up.

'Letter,' he mumbled. 'Forgot.' He fished about in a pocket and withdrew a crumpled envelope. 'Arrived at dawn. Home.'

I opened it as he fell back to sleep.

'The Manor, Ashton Steeple.

Heathcliff, haven't heard from you and there has been no telegram, so I presume you are hard at it, beating the Boche. We go on here. Food is tricky, it's all requisitioned for the war effort. Cook has found interesting ways with turnips. She even added it to the jam; it was frightful.

I've allowed the villagers to use the walled gardens. They're digging their own plots, planting vegetables and whatnots. It's only women, children, and old men. They've raised the age of conscription to fifty-one and many a sixteen-year-old is joining under the blind eye of the recruiting officers.

Cook's sister has come to stay. Meggy Jenkins, a pretty young woman. She's got a little boy, Tommy. He's as bright as a button and chatters away to me. It's really quite refreshing. The father was at the Somme but didn't survive the onslaught, so I said they could remain until a suitable position is found.

I should mention a friend of yours, Dicky Dempster. He was at Ypres. Didn't make it. His parents wrote, there's a memorial service next month. I'll send your usual regrets.

Cyril Fletcher has taken up chess and comes for a game.

*He's ever the gossip, sticking his nose into everybody's business
— but that's the local quack for you. He's been chivvying me
about the cough, I told him I'm going to take up the pipe.
Kill or cure, eh!*

*I've got my mind on a dog. Lady Hamley breeds excel-
lent gun dogs and thinks the next litter will be her best yet.
Golden spaniels, sharp eyes, excellent hearing and totally
fearless - or so she says. I'm putting my name down. It will
be good to have a dog about the place, and when you return,
I plan on making it yours.*

*That's an incentive, my son, it's my way of saying, 'keep
out of trouble'. If your mother were still with us she'd be
writing every day, but there's just me, and you know I'm a
poor correspondent. Doesn't mean you're ever far from my
thoughts though. See it through, then come home. Your old
father misses you. Papa.'*

I pushed the letter back into its envelope and pock-
eted it. A fly buzzed lazily above me as I lay in the straw,
my thoughts in the Cotswolds; a dreaming land of hon-
ey-stone cottages, gentle vales, meandering brooks and
ancient woods.

Dempster dead, damn it. He was clever. One of those
types who'd taken Oxford seriously and actually learned
something. Poor Dicky, I sighed and closed my eyes.

'English?' a voice spoke in my sleep. 'You are
Englishmen?'

I muttered, then blinked awake. A pair of eyes stared
down at me, blue eyes, the colour of cornflowers on a
spring day.

'Wake up,' she made a light touch to my shoulder.
'Who are you?' I was groggy with whisky and weariness.
'I am Eloise.'

CHAPTER 3

'What?' I scrambled to my feet.

'I am come to help you,' she whispered with a French accent. It was rather adorable, actually.

'Why?'

'It was your aeroplane?'

'Yes,' we spoke in undertones, I don't know why; Greggs was sound asleep.

'To return to your army, naturellement.' She tucked a tress of long dark hair behind a small ear. 'What name do you call yourself?'

'Lennox, Major Heathcliff Lennox, but erm... I'm not keen, you know... Just Lennox.'

'Alors, Just Lennox, come please, and your fat friend.'

'Right, erm...Greggs?' I called above his snoring.

He didn't wake. I shook him, that didn't work either.

'You must rouse him.'

'Greggs.' I hissed. He mumbled in his sleep and I noticed there was something odd about the straw he was resting on, it hadn't flattened down, indeed it bulged, which you wouldn't expect when such a bulky chap as Greggs lay on it. I brushed some of the straw aside – there was cloth underneath. I pulled some more away – there was something inside the cloth. I realised what it was and took a smart step backwards.

'What is it?' Eloise leaned forward.

I moved aside to give her a better view.

The byre was dappled with dark shadows and bright sunshine, but the face of the dead man could be made out quite clearly.

'Mon Dieu.' She stared, shock widening her eyes. 'Is this what you did?'

'No, of course not. Never seen him before in my life.'

That didn't seem to convince her, she turned on the heel of her shabby shoe and rushed out.

I rolled Greggs away from the body. He mumbled in his sleep. The corpse wore a German uniform of fine cut and quality. Jack boots, grey breeches, a smart jacket with brass buttons, an embroidered collar and fancy epaulets marked him as a full Colonel. It wasn't unusual to find dead Germans, or dead anything given the slaughter of war, but the upper echelons usually escaped extinction. They were the cause, but they rarely suffered the effect.

Eloise returned with the old farmer and they rattled on in French, I could see by their faces they were as surprised as I was, and I wasn't sure they were convinced of my innocence.

'He's stiff,' I mentioned.

'Pardon?' Eloise replied.

'Like ice, frozen. You know, snow...' I tried to pull myself together, I had a tendency to babble around the fairer sex. 'I mean, erm... I couldn't have killed him, he'd still be warm and... and he's not.'

She came for a closer look at the corpse, then reached to touch the dead man's hand. 'Froid.'

The farmer moved in to make a search of the body. He finished in quick time and rattled off more French.

Eloise translated. 'This man, he is Colonel. And you are correct; he must 'ave been here some time.'

I gazed down at her. Thick, dark lashes framed her intense blue eyes. She had a straight nose, clear creamy skin and fine cheekbones. She wasn't tall, the top of her head barely reached my shoulder. She wore a faded cotton dress, white with small blue flowers, which hung loose on her slender frame.

'How did he die?' I forced myself to concentrate.

She asked the old man another question, he explained with stabbing gestures.

'Bayonet,' she told me.

I thought of the German soldier we'd met, his bayonet had been clean but I recalled the faintest smear of red on the steel.

'Do you know who this Colonel is?' I asked.

'Glessner. We have heard things about him. He is new, from Berlin. A cruel man.' She looked suddenly lost and confused. 'It is so strange; why is he here?'

There wasn't much I could say to that.

The farmer spoke again.

19

Eloise sighed. 'He says we must remove him.'

'If you give me a spade...' I told her.

'A moment, please.' She held up a hand.

More French ensued.

'Monsieur Bandeaux is going to put him in the fosse,' she explained.

'Erm, right.' I was beginning to wish we'd made an escape elsewhere. 'When you say fosse, do you mean ditch?'

'Non, it is pit for... for the excretions, if you know what this is.'

I laughed, her cheeks flushed. The farmer went off and we fell to silence. She seemed rather shy and uncertain, I tried to think of something to say, but couldn't. Greggs snuffled and turned over in the straw, the bull chewed cud, a chicken came and pecked around the dead Colonel's boots.

Just another day in wartime France.

The farmer returned with a wheelbarrow, we heaved the corpse into it. He was stiff as a board, and his arms and legs stuck out at unlikely angles. The old man laid a sack over him, but it was hardly a disguise.

I volunteered to wheel him across the cobbles.

'I will direct you,' Eloise told me. She ran to the other side of the yard and stopped by a pig-sty, then turned to wave frantically at me. 'Vite.'

I vited and made it to her side.

'Maintenant, I go by the hedge, then you come when I blow.' She whistled to demonstrate. It was charming and quite ridiculous.

'Righto,' I waited until I heard her, then made another dash with the cart and corpse.

'This way.' She ran alongside the high hedge, ragged and overgrown, with a few tank-sized holes in it. We came to a large pit, smothered by green algae. It was fed by a terracotta pipe leading from the farmyard, dripping something indescribable.

She pointed. 'In there.'

I tipped him. He didn't roll, just lay on his back staring at the blue sky. His lips held a sneer, his face had turned an unpleasant shade of grey, there was a scar over one eye; he was distinctive and probably distinguished. I heaved and shoved until he slid into the filthy mire and slowly sank. Bubbles rose to the surface, the algae swirled and settled, a lark sang in a neighbouring meadow. We gazed at the fosse, it had all been strange and discordant. Eloise bowed her head and we muttered prayers for the dead, and the living, and for peace.

'Allez,' Eloise murmured, and walked back to the farm.

'Sir,' Greggs had woken, he'd donned his bowler and was brushing straw from his jacket. 'I think we are in need of sustenance. I have experienced unpleasant dreams, they were quite singular.'

I introduced Eloise. He turned pink about the ears and made a courtly bow. She smiled.

'There was a dead…' she began.

'No need for that,' I cut in, not wanting to unsettle the old fellow any further. 'He's right, we need food.'

'Madam Bandeaux will bring what they can spare, but you must be ready. It is a long way to walk.'

'Walk?' Greggs looked aghast.

'Yes, I have a map,' she replied. 'I will come to guide you, do not fear.'

CHAPTER 4

I can't say I was keen on the plan. 'We'll wait until dark.'

'Non, this Colonel is important, they will be making the search for him, they also search for you.' She'd produced a map drawn on a tea cloth. It had been in her undergarments. 'See, this is here.'

We peered at the hand drawn map; it wasn't to any sort of scale. 'Where is here?'

'Near Montsec, east of Saint-Mihiel.'

'Ah,' I muttered, I'd wondered where we were. The dogfight had forced us over enemy lines as I'd attempted to evade the Albatross, but I'd lost all sense of direction during the protracted clash.

'The St Mihiel salient is in enemy territory, sir,' my butler informed me.

'Yes, Greggs I know.' I studied the map. We were within a promontory of the German lines. It was probably only twenty miles or so to the front, but the place would be teaming with soldiers and if they were searching for their dead Colonel, it would make our escape a great deal more fraught.

'We go, please.' She gave an uncertain smile.

I gazed down at her. 'No, not you.'

'I'll take the map, miss,' Greggs tugged it gently from her hands.

'I come.' She was insistent. 'I am guiding you.'

'No,' I countered.

'I know the route, it is not by the roads.' She raised her chin in determination. 'You cannot find your way without me.'

I hesitated, I didn't want to put her in danger, but realised she was right.

'Fine, but we should have a plan. I'll give you my gun, and if we're about to be caught, you can shoot us.'

'Non,' she balked.

'Sir!' Greggs objected.

'Not to kill, just pretend you're trying to capture us.' Really, why did I have to explain everything?

'This idea is risible.' She wasn't convinced.

By the look on Greggs' face, he wasn't either.

I gave up. Besides, I'd thought of something else. 'Shouldn't we wear French clothes?'

Eloise wasn't impressed by that, either. 'Non, you are too big.'

'Nonsense, not all French are short chaps, I've met any number…'

'This is true, but the Germans believe all Frenchmen are short, so they will stop you anyway,' she explained. 'It is no matter, we go by the trees and not be seen.'

The wizened dame reappeared, bearing a small sack.

She opened it to show us. It was filled with the type of goodies only French farms are capable of producing. She chattered away as she handed it to Greggs. He replied with a smile and raised his bowler hat. She was charmed and grinned at him; neither of them understanding a word the other uttered.

'Alors,' the farmer raced in, alarm in his face and voice. He held onions and threw two on the floor and stomped on them, then kicked them into the straw.

'What the...?' I exclaimed.

'For to disguise the scent of the dead man,' Eloise told me, then fired questions at the farmer, who replied with dramatic gesticulations toward the meadows.

'Damn,' I muttered. It didn't take a genius to work out that the enemy was close by.

'Venez,' Eloise called and ran from the byre.

We followed, we could hear shouting coming from the direction of the hill and we raced behind the farmstead, alongside a broken fence and into a copse of tall trees.

'Down, Greggs,' I hissed and took the sack and map from his hands.

The poor chap had barely made it to his knees when Eloise was back on her feet.

'They have dogs,' Eloise hissed.

'We need somewhere to hide,' I replied in a low voice.

Greggs groaned.

'Come.' Eloise waved her hand.

'No, wait,' I caught her. 'They mustn't find you with us, go back.'

'The dogs will catch me,' she whispered. 'And I made a promise...'

'Promised who?' I asked, but the baying of the hounds grew louder and she dashed off without answering.

I grabbed Greggs and bundled him along as best he could manage. We ran to the vines and along the length of their lines until we reached the edge of a forest. Eloise ran straight to a thicket of brambles. They were in bloom, exuding a sweet scent and buzzing with bees. She picked up a fallen branch and used it to raise the thick briars and wriggled her way in. I had a harder time pushing Greggs through the gap, but we made it.

She laughed quietly, her face was alight with adventure. 'I hid here as a child.'

'It's a good place,' I whispered.

'Are we staying here, sir?' Greggs asked

'For the moment,' I replied.

There was a hollow in the centre of the thicket, the brambles had grown over a clump of shrubs to form a thorny canopy above. I could tell by the various holes dug out, and hairs caught on barbs, that it belonged to badgers. They were nocturnal and shy so wouldn't bother us and their scent might even be enough to mask our own.

'There are boiled eggs, bread, cheese and ham, sir.' Greggs had been inspecting the contents of the sack. 'And onions.'

'Take one onion each,' Eloise whispered. 'And wipe it on, then throw the rest aside.'

She peeled a fat onion, rubbed it on her arms and legs, then threw it into the surrounding briars.

I sighed, it really was a day for unexpected delights.

Greggs couldn't quite bring himself to do it, so Eloise did the honours for him. He sat there looking like a stricken spaniel, his hangdog eyes drooping with fatigue and dejection.

We waited, listening as the soldiers shouted to each other. We even heard the panting of dogs at one point; but the combined stink of badgers and onions must have overwhelmed the hounds' sensitive noses, because they didn't try to enter the thicket. Another hour ticked by in silence, apart from the hum of bees and the occasional scrabbling of mice.

'May we eat, now?' Greggs asked.

'Oui,' Eloise replied with a smile.

We tucked in, the strain of the day and the frisson of excitement adding to our hunger. It tasted heavenly, smoked ham, soft cheese, boiled eggs and fresh bread. We all felt better for the picnic, despite the peculiar circumstances.

'We stay here until nightfall,' I told her.

She nodded agreement. 'I think so, there is too much soldiers now.'

'And you will return to the farm.'

Greggs had turned over, put his hat aside and his hands under his head. He began snoring, I hoped it couldn't be heard beyond the thicket.

'Not yet. I told you, I show you the way, I have promised,' she replied. She was sitting next to me, almost touching, her thin arms wrapped around her legs.

'Promised who?' I'd tried to ask the same question earlier.

'Myself,' she whispered. 'My husband was with Les Dame Blanches, he died for them. Now I help in his place.'

I knew of Les Dames Blanches, they were one of the largest resistance groups in Belgium and France.

'I'm sorry,' I spoke in a low tone. 'Have you done this before?'

She raised her eyes to look at me. 'Non, there are not so many Englishmen now. But I did blow up a train.'

'All on your own?' I teased her.

She laughed. 'With the others. They are very practiced.'

'You seem rather young for wrecking trains,' I said.

'I am twenty-one. It is a good age.' She glanced at me again. 'What age are you?'

'Twenty five, nearly twenty six.'

'So, you are old man.'

I laughed. I could smell her hair; lavender, rosemary and thyme. Her fine-boned fingers were grimy, soil under short nails, small ears, white teeth, pretty lips. I watched her; her uncertainty, her resolution and her courage.

'Do you have children?'

'Non,' she shook her head. 'There was no time. And you, you are married?'

'No,' I replied. 'I haven't met many girls. I went to boarding school, all-boys and, erm, well, they didn't allow… I mean obviously there weren't any….' I broke off to stop the babbling.

She laughed. 'You must be rich, if you can fly the areoplane.'

I paused at that. 'We were, but my mother died and my father rather went to pieces. It all just slipped away, really.'

'But how did you learn to fly if you do not have money.'

'Our family have money, some of them anyway. My Uncle offered the funds, he thought I'd enjoy it. Then the war came, so I joined up and carried on flying.'

'And you want to continue to be a pilot?' She asked. 'When the war ends?'

'Erm, I've no idea,' I'd never thought that far. 'My family don't really have jobs.'

She laughed at that. 'But you have muscles, you are strong, you must do something.'

'I play sport – rugby, cricket, and I hunt and fish – things like that.' I didn't want to talk about me. 'What about you? Did you grow up here?'

She nodded. 'In the village, it is not far from the farm. Everyone is like family.'

'Did you have work before the war?'

'My Papa sold milk in St Miheil, and cheese. I helped.'

That made me grin, the locals always brought milk to the airfields. A farmer would arrive with a handcart bearing a copper churn. There was often a pretty girl in attendance, which attracted the chaps like bees to honey. She would ladle the frothy milk out into our tin mugs while we tried to chat to her in execrable French.

'So you're a milk maid?' I smiled.

She laughed. 'Non. After my father died, I was a teacher of little children. This is what I will be again, one day.'

'What about your mother, or...?'

'She was killed. My parents rest in the cimetière with my brothers.'

I cudgelled my mind for soft words, but nothing seemed adequate, so I reached out my hand and took hers. She didn't object.

A tremor shook the ground. A shell had landed somewhere. Neither of us flinched.

'Far away,' I muttered.

'In the valley, it is the same each day,' she replied quietly.

A louder sound rattled from the forest just beyond the thicket. 'Damn,' I swore to myself, pushing her to the ground and lying on top of her.

'Machine guns,' I hissed.

She didn't reply. I could hear her breathing, rapid and frightened.

Neither of us moved. Greggs burbled in his sleep.

We remained motionless for some time, then she turned over to tuck her head under my chin. I nuzzled her hair until she fell asleep, wrapped in my arms. I lay awake, listening to her every sigh, her every breath. It was absurd to feel that way about someone after so short a time, but I knew that I'd protect her with my life if necessary.

CHAPTER 5

It was dusk when she woke, the ground growing cold beneath us. I hadn't moved for fear of disturbing her, she gazed at me, I kissed her gently, then she sighed and whispered my name.

'We should be going,' I murmured, but remained where I was.

She gave a quiet laugh. 'It is time.'

I sat up, listening intently to the sound of the world outside. Birds sang, full of that joyous season, and an indication that the forest was free of soldiers and hunting hounds. I crawled from our hiding hole and cautiously rose to my feet. The air was crisp and clear; it felt a million miles from the war although I knew it wasn't far at all.

'Hurry,' I called in a low tone.

Eloise must have had some trouble rousing Greggs because it was a few minutes before they emerged. He was still clutching his hat. His butlering togs were crumpled, muddied and tagged with ragged tears. The poor chap looked dreadfully dishevelled.

'We'll find a boat,' I promised, although I hadn't a clue how to go about it.

'It may be possible, I know of one' Eloise whispered. 'But we must join the river further south.'

She led off into the forest and we made our way as the night grew quieter and darkness fell.

It was a long, tedious affair. We followed animal trails where we could, other times we had to push through brush and undergrowth. By dawn, my poor butler was all in. We sat, bone tired and aching on a rise at the edge of the tree line, gazing through a fine mist at the winding River Meuse below.

'Slow flowing,' I remarked, watching ducks drift past a vacant jetty which jutted out into the water.

'Oui, but it is wide, with places to hide.' Eloise indicated the thick reed beds filling the shallows.

'There don't appear to be any boats,' Greggs observed.

'They come,' Eloise replied. 'We wait.'

I tried not to think about breakfast, or the lack of it.

We heard the bleating first; sheep in a flock coming along the broad river bank. Men whistled, dogs ran around the herd to keep them moving at a trot, then steered them toward the long expanse of the jetty. It was a sturdy affair, built with thick planks, a gate at the end and robust rails to prevent the unwary plunging into the water. We waited while the men and beasts arranged themselves along the dock. An open decked barge chugged into view, emerging from the mist with plumes of black smoke rising from its stubby funnel.

'Allons y,' Eloise strolled down as though we were merely passengers waiting for a ferry.

Greggs brushed away the worst of the mud from his clothes, wiped his bowler on his sleeve and put it on his head.

'Ready?' I asked.

'Indeed sir.'

We followed her to the dock where she'd started an animated discussion with the shepherds. They were all old men, the youngsters would have gone to war. Phlegmatic, unhurried and amiable, they nodded agreement to the uncommon request.

'They only go to the front line, not beyond,' Eloise explained as we stood surrounded by sheep. 'Then a waterman will carry you in the dark, back to your people.'

'Come with us,' I urged her.

She laughed, her cheek was streaked with grime, her hair tumbling about her face in long tendrils. 'Non, I promised to help you escape, but I stay here to help the others.'

I wasn't going to argue, but I wasn't prepared to leave her either, not when I'd only just found her. Greggs was helped onto the barge first and told to get down amongst the beasts. He refused, he went to sit on a seat at the bow, an unlikely figurehead in the thinning fog.

I helped bundle the sheep onto the open deck. I was just handing a squirming lamb to one of the weathered shepherds when the howl of dogs made us all swing around.

'Down,' I yelled.

Greggs tumbled off his perch in shock as Eloise slid off the dock and into the water, then ducked beneath the planking. I vaulted the rail to land with a splash and swam to join her.

'Hush,' she hissed.

We watched as a soldier in grey uniform ran from the forest and across the wide, grassy bank as the first dog broke through the trees. A dozen more raced in a pack behind, followed by yelling soldiers with rifles on their backs. The hunted man pounded into the water, mouth gaping, eyes wide with terror, he ploughed towards the boat, his hand outstretched. A sudden staccato of machine gun fire burst from the bank and the man jerked as the bullets hit. He span around, thrown sideways then fell into an eddy of his own making. No-one on the barge or dock spoke a word. They just looked on in grim horror as the dead man floated away in a bloom of red blood.

Barking ferociously, the dogs raced towards me and Eloise. They were Alsatians, more black than brown and they knew we were prey. We ducked down in the water and held our breath. Whistles and shouts called them back, their handlers had already got their man and assumed the dogs were after the frantic sheep. We waited, freezing cold and shivering, as the Germans turned away to follow the corpse drifting downstream.

'Sir.' Greggs had been watching from just behind the boat rail. 'That was the soldier to whom we gave the sausages.'

'I know.' I sighed a sharp breath. 'And if you don't get down they'll be using you as target practice next.'

He muttered something inaudible and sank below the rail.

Eloise was shaken, I drew her to me, hugged her to my chest and kissed her gently on the lips.

'I'm not leaving you,' I insisted.

'Do not say this.'

'Why not? What is left for you here?'

'My...' her voice trailed off. 'My country.'

'It will still be here.' I told her. 'We'll come back when it's over.'

She raised a hand to wipe her cheek. 'It is my duty.'

'No, it will make no difference, the war will go on with or without you.'

She looked away.

'Eloise, please,' I pressured her. 'It may be our only chance.'

She stared up into my eyes, then gave the faintest of nods.

I settled her among the sheep then helped finish the loading. We steamed off in the opposite direction to the soldiers, for which I was grateful. The old shepherds shared bread and cheese with us and we sat on the deck, eating among the beasts. We were dripping, dishevelled and dirty, but the sun shone and we still had our freedom and our lives. Greggs ate breakfast and afterwards he had to lie down, poor chap, his stoic front dissolved.

The boat puttered along the river, hissing with steam, I dozed on the deck with Eloise in my arms, until a familiar stench woke me. I'd been to the front; it wound for hundreds of miles through France, but the stink remained the same wherever it was. Ordure, decay, and the putrid reek of death.

I sat up, I could see it in the distance, beyond the shambles of a semi-derelict town; towers of wood, field guns, howitzers, anti-aircraft posts, lorries, carts, bunkers, buildings, soldiers and a sea of mud.

We were passing the last shreds of grassy fields when the barge slowed and began to drift toward the high bank.

'Why are they stopping?' Eloise scrambled to her feet and went to speak to the nearest man.

'What's happening?' I went to her side.

The boat-master came over, a diminutive chap with a pipe and beret, he explained quietly to Eloise.

'Non.' She objected and began to argue with him.

His eyes went from me to Eloise. He made a slow reply and shook his head.

'What is it?'

Her gaze fell to the deck, then she looked up at me. 'I have to go back, they are making me get off.'

'No,' I stared around at the men's faces, resolute and unflinching.

'They say there is too much risk. If I am caught with you, I will be tortured, then I will be shot.'

They were right and I was wrong for wanting to keep her with me. Words of persuasion formed on my lips, but I bit them back. There was no choice, I knew it, but I wanted to rail against the bloody madness that had forced us into this situation. I nodded in mute assent and looked away.

The barge bumped up against the bank, Eloise waited motionless, tears forming in her eyes.

'I'll come back for you,' I told her, then lifted her into my arms to step with her off the boat.

She wept as I carried her up to the meadow and put her down on the grass.

'Do you promise?' She whispered.

'I promise.' I stroked damp tresses away from her face.

Teardrops ran down her cheeks. I cradled her, cursing under my breath against the insanity of the world, before I finally let her go. Greggs had followed and was clutching a bunch of wild flowers he'd found among the spring grass. They were cornflowers, he gave them to her with a kindly smile then returned to the boat.

The master blew the whistle, I held Eloise in my arms once more, whispered my love into her ears, kissed her, then turned to leave.

She remained unmoving on the bank, the flowers clutched to her breast, I stayed at the rail and watched until I lost sight of her.

EPILOGUE

We were hidden in a sheep shed for two more nights until a volunteer was found to smuggle us through the formidable defences. We lay at the bottom of an open rowing boat, covered by an oilskin, and were paddled through the German front line in streaming rain under a pitch-black sky. Fear, cold and hunger shook us to our bones, but we made it.

Days later we were greeted with good humour and hot tea when we were delivered to our troops. The enemy offensive, led by the elite storm troopers, failed in the north-west. It rang the death knell for German ambitions and put them on the defensive from that moment on. Greggs and I returned to Etiez as part of RAF support to the burgeoning American forces.

In early September, General Pershing started the first American-led offensive, the opening attack was launched on the Saint-Miheil salient. I led my squadron as part of air support. The strike was made on all sides, it was short, brutal and bloody. Within days, the allies took control of the area at a cost of 6,500 lives and many thousand more casualties, of which I was one. I was hit by a bullet in the thigh, which put me in hospital for weeks.

Greggs was as indefatigable as I, in the search for Eloise. We tried every avenue, but couldn't find any trace of her in the chaotic aftermath. Armistice was declared just as word reached me that my father was dying. I'd barely recovered from my injury, but was determined to fly back and spend his last days together at our home, the Manor at Ashton Steeple.

News of Eloise reached me as 1918 drew to a close.

I kept my promise. Greggs and I did return, we took flowers to put on the grave of the girl with eyes the colour of cornflowers in spring.

The memory of love never fades, it forms a shadow in the heart and endures until we die.

Demain, dès l'aube, à l'heure où blanchit la campagne,
Je partirai. Vois-tu, je sais que tu m'attends.
J'irai par la forêt, j'irai par la montagne.
Je ne puis demeurer loin de toi plus longtemps.

From the poem by *Victor Hugo*

Here's the full Heathcliff Lennox series list with links to each book on Audible, Amazon and all good book stores.

Book 1: *Murder at Melrose Court*
Book 2: *The Black Cat Murders*
Book 3: *The Curse of Braeburn Castle*
Book 4: *Death in Damascus*
Book 5: *The Monks Hood Murders*
Book 6: *The Tomb of the Chatelaine*
Book 7: *The Mystery of Montague Morgan* (Previewed for Christmas 2021)

More books are planned! And there are Audible versions read by Sam Dewhurst-Phillips, who is outstanding, it's just like listening to a radio play. All of these can be found on Amazon, Audible and Apple Books. To find them on Amazon, just click on one of the book links above and opt for Audio.

***

I do hope you enjoyed your book. Would you like to take a look at the Heathcliff Lennox website? You'll find portraits of Lennox, Swift, Greggs, Foggy, Tubbs, Persi and Tommy Jenkins on the 'World of Lennox' page. There are also inspirations for the books, plus occasional newsletters with updates and free giveaways.

You can find the Heathcliff Lennox Readers Club, and more, at https://karenmenuhin.com/

***

Reviews are always appreciated and kind words go a long way. If you're upset by anything, please let me know and I'll be very happy to listen, we all learn from each other.

You can contact me here:
karenmenuhinauthor@gmail.com

I'd love to hear from you and will always reply.

Karen Baugh Menuhin

A little about Karen Baugh Menuhin

1920s, Cozy crime, Traditional Detectives, Downton Abbey – I love them!

Along with my family, my dog and my cat.

At 60 I decided to write, I don't know why but suddenly the stories came pouring out, along with the characters. Eccentric Uncles, stalwart butlers, idiosyncratic servants, machinating Countesses, and the hapless Major Heathcliff Lennox.

A whole world built itself upon the page and I just followed along...

An itinerate traveller all my life. I grew up in the military, often on RAF bases but preferring to be in the countryside when we could. I adore whodunnits.

I have two amazing sons – Jonathan and Sam Baugh and their wives, Laura and Wendy, and five grandchildren, Charlie, Joshua, Isabella-Rose, Scarlett and Hugo.

I am married to Krov, my wonderful husband, who is a retired film maker and eldest son of the violinist, Yehudi Menuhin. We live in the Cotswolds.

For more information my address is:
karenmenuhinauthor@gmail.com

Made in the USA
Coppell, TX
22 July 2021